SO YOU WANT TO BE A
ROMAN SOLDIER?

Written by
GEORGIA AMSON-BRADSHAW

Illustrated by
TAKAYO AKIYAMA

Inspired by the book *Legionary* by
PHILIP MATYSZAK

Thames & Hudson

So you want to be a Roman soldier?
© 2019 Thames & Hudson Ltd, London

Based on the book by Philip Matyszak
Legionary © 2009 Thames & Hudson Ltd, London

Illustrations © 2019 Takayo Akiyama

Abridged from the original by Georgia Amson-Bradshaw
Designed by Belinda Webster

First published in 2019 in hardcover in the United States of America by
Thames & Hudson Inc., 500 Fifth Avenue, New York, New York 10110

www.thamesandhudsonusa.com

Library of Congress Control Number 2019931889

ISBN 978-0-500-65183-4

Printed and bound in China by Everbest Printing Co. Ltd

At the history museum...

5

7

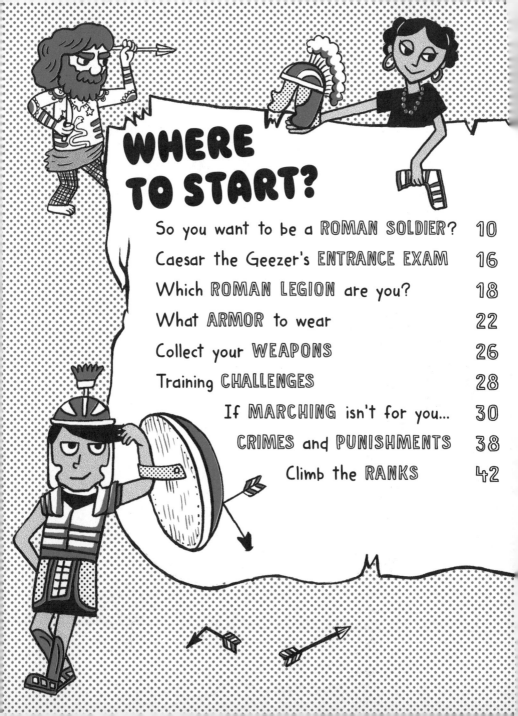

WHERE TO START?

SO YOU WANT TO BE A ...
ROMAN SOLDIER?

Hello my dears! I'm JUNIA. So, you're interested in becoming Roman soldiers? It's a tough job. But I'll leave it to you to decide. Here's the information you need.

I know I'm going to be awesome at this.

I'll take that!

CAREER ADVICE

100 CE

Do Mom and Dad know you're signing up?

THE EMPIRE NEEDS YOU!

Have you got what it takes to join the most DEADLY FIGHTING FORCE the world has ever seen?

A career with the ROMAN ARMY will bring you glory, excitement and adventure, as well as a range of other excellent perks!

SIGN UP TO BE PART OF THE 100 CE INTAKE TODAY!

VOTE FOR ME!

I'VE KILLED LOADS OF PEOPLE!

Sign up today so you can...

BECOME POWERFUL

Being a Roman soldier is a very good career choice if one day you'd like to be a politician.

Most of the emperors of Rome have been soldiers, and during the Roman Republic of 509–27 BCE voters preferred their leaders to have proven their loyalty to their country by slaying at least a few enemies on the battlefield.

EARN MONEY

Every new recruit is given money to cover the cost of traveling to their new training base.

You can travel first class like an officer and arrive broke, or hitchhike and arrive with a full piggy bank.

TRAVEL THE WORLD

International travel is a perk of the job of being a legionary (Roman soldier). You might find yourself sent anywhere in the empire.

Kate, where is Dacia?

No idea.

Of course, some posts are more desirable than others: get the low-down on the best legions to join on page 18.

RETIRE RICH

If you do manage to make it to the end of your service alive, the Roman army offers great retirement pay, and military veterans are well-respected members of society.

ROMAN SOLDIER APPLICATION FORM

Check all boxes that apply:

1. I AM ROMAN

If you want to be a ROMAN SOLDIER you have to be a ROMAN CITIZEN. That means you can't be someone's property, and you can't be from any of the conquered territories in the empire. If you aren't a ROMAN CITIZEN you can try and get citizenship by doing a favor for someone important.

2. I AM AT LEAST 5 FOOT 8 INCHES TALL

You have to be a MINIMUM HEIGHT to enter. Having said that, exceptions can be made for particularly sturdy individuals.

3. I HAVE ALL MY BODY PARTS

You must be fully fit and healthy to join the Roman Army, so absolutely NO MISSING fingers, thumbs, feet, arms, heads, etc.

4. I AM NOT MARRIED

Only SINGLES ALLOWED in the army! However, if you do have a spouse whom you'd like to give the heave-ho, joining the army serves as a declaration of divorce.

5. I HAVE GOOD EYESIGHT

IF YOU CAN'T READ THIS, FORGET IT.

Now, please attach your letter of recommendation from a local bigwig or former soldier: references will be checked!

To join the ranks, you'll first need to pass Caesar the Geezer's...

ENTRANCE EXAM

If you pass the test, you'll then be sworn in to the army by saying the MILITARY OATH. This is it—your final moment of freedom! If you change your mind after this, you'll be executed if you try to leave.

DROP AND GIVE ME TWENTY, MAGGOTS!

!!!

I solemnly swear to follow my commander, obey all orders, serve Rome faithfully and respect the law for the next 25 years until the end of my time of duty!

Yeah, if a PUNY WEAKLING like you LIVES THAT LONG,

HA HA HA!

LOOK AT ME!

Hehe...

Well, I've never seen a birthmark like that before.

After the SWEARING IN, your name will be recorded along with any identifying marks or scars that could help identify your dead body on the battlefield. You'll also be given a small lead tablet to wear around your neck with your name on it.

YOU PASSED!
You are now a shiny new recruit in the Roman army. You'll travel to your army barracks—where you'll meet your UNIT who will be your pals for the next 25 years.

Hope you like each other!

Hi, I'm Claudius, your bunk mate!

I'm Eddie...

With so many legions in the Roman army that you could join, you'll want to make sure you find the one that suits you best.

Try this QUIZ to find out...

WHICH ROMAN LEGION ARE YOU?

1. PICK A FOOTWEAR LOOK

A

Leather shoes with wool socks

B

Fancy sandals with nice leatherwork

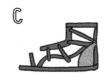

C

Simple lightweight sandals

D

Mid-calf red leather boots

2. PICK A WEEKEND ACTIVITY

A

Going for a hike

B

Going on a romantic date

C

Doing some painting

D

Having a huge feast

3. PICK A FAVORITE DISH

A

Roast mutton
and grain

B

Grain porridge
with figs

C

Baked grain

D

Stewed grain

4. PICK A LUCKY CHARM

A

Lion's head

B

Diving dolphin

C

Clenched fist

D

Golden boot

5. PICK A HOLIDAY DESTINATION

A

Northern Britain

B
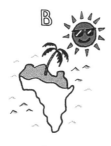
North Africa

C

Germany

D

France

COUNT UP YOUR A, B, C AND D ANSWERS. CHECK THE RESULTS ON THE NEXT PAGE >>>

QUIZ RESULTS:

IF YOU CHOSE MOSTLY A's
YOU'RE GOING TO: XX VALERIA VICTRIX

Softie southerners need not apply to this legion of legends stationed in NORTHERN BRITAIN. After several successful wars against the Picts* these brave boys spend their time on guard in the freezing fog of soggy Britain, and generally being super tough.

* from modern-day Scotland

MOSTLY B's
III AUGUSTA

The legion for lovers, this is the place to be if you want to kick back in sunny NORTH AFRICA and go on romantic dates with beautiful locals. Occasional fighting with Berbers.

MOSTLY C's
X GEMINA

You're obviously a creative type, so head to the area around the RIVER RHINE in Germany and have a go at carpentry. The legion is currently building a series of wooden forts along the river.

MOSTLY D's
VIII AUGUSTA

You live for the finer things in life, so get on down to ARGENTORATUM (Strasbourg in France). You won't be expected to do much in the legion except eat the excellent local cuisine and drink wine. What could be better?

LEGION NAMES

There were about 30 different legions in 100 CE. They had different names, depending on which emperor founded them or what their motto was. The legions named AUGUSTA were started by the emperor Augustus. VALERIA VICTRIX means "Valor (bravery) Victorious."

Because there was more than one legion with the same name, they were numbered using Roman numerals. "III" means 3 and "X" means 10.

"Legion" is where the name "legionary" comes from. It's another name for "Roman soldier."

Learn how to DECODE the other Roman numbers on page 93.

METELLA'S GUIDE
WHAT TO WEAR IN THE ARMY

Hi new recruits! You'll want to look good for your first day in your legion. Let me show you how to create a stylish everyday army look!

TIP #1

You want to start off with your TUNIC, which is like a simple dress. What material you use is up to you, but I would personally choose WOOL if you're stationed somewhere cold, and LINEN if you're somewhere warm.

Classic army style is to have the hemline above the knee, and to cinch the tunic in at the waist with a simple belt.

Your unit will probably have a color that everyone wears—red is really in with a lot of legions because the dye that makes it, called "MADDER," is cheap and it hides bloodstains really nicely.

Angus, which is better?

The one with less stains.

22

TIP #2

ARMOR not only looks cool, but is also super handy for not getting stabbed during battle.

Most legionaries wear figure-hugging "lobster-style" armor made of metal bands mounted onto a leather frame.

STEEL is considered better than iron if you can get it, but whichever you choose you'll need to polish it often. Use grease to keep it from getting rusty and going a yucky shade of orange. Not nice.

YOU SHOULD SERIOUSLY CONSIDER PAYING—OR FORCING—SOMEONE TO POLISH YOUR ARMOR FOR YOU.

Lobster-style **ARMOR** is made up of 34 separate pieces which all need to be taken apart, polished band by band, and fixed back together again. I mean, as glamorous as the results might be, that's a sweaty piece of work! And there's no such thing as a dry cleaner in 100 CE.

23

TIP #3

Next up you want to grab a pair of CALIGAE, or leather hobnailed sandals. The metal hobnails make this a really practical choice for wearing around the camp, as well as on long marches, as they give you super grip on muddy ground.

They are also great if you need to kick someone in the face! If it's cold, you can accessorize with a pair of WOOL SOCKS. Cute!

TIP #4

Finally, your HELMET! Size really matters when it comes to headgear, so make sure you get one that fits well. Otherwise it will slip down over your eyes or stay perched on top of your head!

The BRIM on the back protects your neck, and the CHEEK FLAPS can deflect stones and arrows.

I'd better take it off...

Don't wear PLUMES on your helmet in battle. They might have been fashionable in Caesar's time but not any more in 100 CE. Save them for a special parade.

TIP #5

Check yourself out in the mirror...

Eddie, you look **SO COOL!**

TA-DA!
LOVE THIS LOOK!
Read about accessories on page 26.

COLLECT YOUR WEAPONS

As well as your clothes, you'll need to get tools of the trade. The trade being killing and/or injuring people. The tools being weapons. The most important weapon in battle is...

...your SWORD, called a "gladius" (which is where "gladiator" comes from). Your sword should have the following features:

I name you... STAB-A-TRON 6000!

STRONG BLADE
A strong, sharp steel blade is needed for all the stabby stuff.

NON-SLIP HANDLE
During battle your hands are going to be very slippery, either with blood or with sweat. A nice bone handle will stop it from flying out of your hand.

BLOOD
Ideally your enemy's and not your own.

WELL-FITTING SCABBARD
Your scabbard is for holding your sword. It shouldn't be too tight or you won't be able to whip your sword out quickly. It also shouldn't be so loose that it rattles around.

The next most important item is your SHIELD. This chunk of curved wood with a handle on the back can be used to deflect arrows, or for punching. It's like an absolutely massive knuckleduster.

A short DAGGER, called a "pugio," is good for killing people and cutting up apples. Kitchen cutlery is not recommended as a substitute.

Finally, grab a SPEAR, called a "pilum." This is used for long-distance fights: you throw it at your enemies in battle. It is deliberately designed to break after one use so the enemy can't throw it back.

Now that you look like a ROMAN SOLDIER, it's time to start acting like one...

LISTEN UP MAGGOTS!
Time to see what you're made of...

In order to prove that you're ready for the real fighting, you need to complete some...

ARMY TRAINING CHALLENGES!!!

CHALLENGE NO. 1:
MARCHING

First, a little warm-up for you. You have to walk 40 miles in 12 hours, wearing full armor. Oh, and in perfect time with the rest of the recruits, too—no excuses.

I thought challenges were meant to be FUN.

CHALLENGE NO. 2:
BATTLING A POST

You're too wimpy to fight any REAL people, so let's see your moves fighting a wooden post. I expect the post will win.

CHALLENGE NO. 3:

GETTING HIT BY A SPEAR

My favorite challenge: you have to learn to throw your pilum, but also how to duck it. Watch out— I throw fast!

Catch it with your hand, not your head.

CHALLENGE NO. 4:

GYMNASTICS

Try to jump over a vaulting horse while wearing your armor. I doubt you weak losers will even make it off the ground. But if you do manage it, you might be allowed to join the cavalry...

CHALLENGE NO. 5:

DRILL

Your unit has to learn to change position on the battlefield IN PERFECT TIME. Watch your step—because I will be, too!

If marching isn't for you, why not...

JOIN THE CAVALRY

If you can stay upright while strapped to a moving animal, and don't barf at the smell of horse poop, the cavalry could be for you.

PROS

✔ You don't have to walk.
✔ Did I mention that you don't have to walk?
✔ In desperate times, horses have a lot of meat on them...

CONS

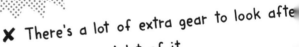

✗ There's a lot of extra gear to look after
✗ Horse poop. A lot of it.
✗ Your enemies all have better cavalry than the Romans.

CAVALRY GEAR AND EQUIPMENT

JAVELINS
For launching at enemies before hand-to-hand combat.

SHINY STUFF
Medallions and buckles to glint in the sun and look pretty.

CAVALRY HELMET
Provides extra protection all-around, to stop the rider getting stabbed in the throat from below.

SADDLE
oesn't have stirrups for your feet, so soldiers ust develop thighs strong nough to crack walnuts.

SWORD AND SHIELD
A cavalry sword, called a "spatha," is a bit longer. A cavalry shield is smaller and oval.

The army understands that not everyone is lucky enough to be born a Roman citizen. Or talented enough to ride a horse. That's fine! The army welcomes all sorts. You will just get paid less and be more likely to get killed.

IF YOU'RE NOT A ROMAN CITIZEN, AND YOU CAN'T RIDE A HORSE, YOU CAN...

JOIN THE AUXILIA

The role of the AUXILIA is to "help." In other words, it's your job to get stuck on the enemies' swords first.

PROS

Don't worry darling, I'm in the auxilia— I'll never leave!

✔ Units usually stay local. If you're lucky, you'll do less dangerous work, like being the muscle for tax collectors.

Pay your taxes or I'm going to have to hurt you.

✔ Life is less strict than it is in the legions. By staying local, auxiliaries can have a life outside work.

CONS

✘ Auxilia get paid less than legionaries and usually have to bring their own ride.

✘ You are easy to replace and will be made to do more dangerous work like being the first to face your enemy.

✘ If your unit in the auxilia does move, it'll be pretty permanent.

Ha, yes babe. You know how I said I wouldn't leave...

I'll whisk those pesky Picts into a bloody mousse!

Some Roman citizens join the auxilia because they are skilled with a weapon that isn't standard equipment. Why learn how to kill with a sword when you're more skilled at wielding a whisk?

JOIN THE NAVY

If you've been longing for adventure, what better choice than to sail the seven* seas in the navy. Arrr!

PROS

✔ You'll travel to exotic locations.

✔ You'll fight pirates and use fun weapons like flaming catapults.

*In Roman times, the seven seas were the waters around Europe, North Africa and the Middle East. Throughout history, as more parts of the globe were discovered, the phrase began to refer to other oceans.

CONS

✗ Other parts of the Roman army hate the navy. It has a bad reputation for sinking its own ships. In the first Punic war 250,000 soldiers drowned before they even faced their enemy.

No! I'm too good-looking to die!

✗ Rowing a trireme (a Roman warship) is a lot of hard work. But it does give you great arm muscles.

EVERY YOUNG SOLDIER DREAMS
OF ONE DAY BEING PROMOTED TO...

THE PRAETORIAN GUARD

These are the elite troops who work as personal bodyguards to the emperor—and it's the cushiest job in town.

PRAETORIANS are based in Rome, where the emperor lives. When on duty at the palace, they wear comfortable togas instead of armor.

PROS

✔ You can quit early after only 16 years on the job. At the end of your service, you can go on to become a CENTURION in a regular legion, or take your cash reward and start a new life (see page 44).

✔ The pay is higher and the barracks are more comfy.

✔ You get a nice fat wad of cash every time a new emperor takes over, because...

...the emperor needs the loyal support of the Praetorians to stay in power. The emperor will do anything to keep the Praetorians happy.

I do decree the following: all Praetorians will be given another pay rise, and must henceforth all be addressed as "You Absolute Legend."

Foolish emperors like CALIGULA, who made the mistake of upsetting the Praetorians, will meet a pointy end.

You forgot my birthday?!

And that's it! There are

NO CONS

to joining the

PRAETORIAN GUARD.

37

CRIMES AND PUNISHMENTS

The Roman army isn't summer camp! There are strict rules, enforced with a range of punishments from minor to deadly.

MINOR PUNISHMENTS

★ The punishment that fits almost any crime is being whacked with a stick or hit on the head. This punishment can be adjusted to suit the crime depending on the strength of the whacks.

★ Being assigned extra duties such as cleaning out stables and bathrooms. This punishment can be given some extra spice by forcing the legionary to wear their tunic in the style of a woman's dress.

For serious crimes, there are:

MAJOR PUNISHMENTS

★ You will lose your rank and privileges. Having a high rank gets you out of grunt work. So being demoted to a general dogsbody really stinks. As does being sent to join a useless unit.

★ You'll receive a beating in front of the rest of your unit. This is much more serious than being whacked with a stick, but not as bad as being...

★ **BEATEN TO DEATH**
This punishment is rather permanent. Avoid being this naughty at all costs.

JOINT PUNISHMENT

If your entire unit disappoints the General, there are a range of joint punishments you could suffer.

DECIMATION

If a unit flees from battle, they might be "decimated" for their cowardice. This is where every tenth man is killed, either by being clubbed to death or beheaded.

By 100 CE, decimation is less common.
You're more likely to be treated to one of the following...

EAT PET FOOD

If your unit is cowardly, you'll be fed barley for dinner instead of wheat. (Barley was generally used to feed animals.)

Ughhh...

SLEEP OUTSIDE

If your unit has been cowardly, you'll be made to pitch your tents outside the main camp walls.

It's less safe, it's uncomfortable and you'll have to stay there until you demonstrate bravery in battle.

I think there is a tiger outside.

You're fired!

YOU'RE FIRED!

If the emperor decides your unit is simply too useless to be in the army, he will banish you all, full stop. You will be too embarrassed to show your face in public ever again.

PINK SLIP

CLIMB THE RANKS

Don't get your hopes up about being promoted. Most soldiers retire at the same rank they entered the army. However, special skills or a bit of bribery can help you climb the ranks.

LOWEST OF THE LOW

Unless you come from a rich family who tosses the higher-ups some money before you join, you'll start at the bottom as a **MUNIFEX**.

Good day sir!

A munifex has no rank or privileges, and is given all the heavy lifting and toilet-cleaning jobs. Even a pack donkey has a higher status.

Hmmm, I think that's how you spell "assassinate."

SEMI-SKILLED

Once you're fully-trained, you can use a special skill to become an IMMUNE. Immunes do specialist tasks such as record-keeping, plumbing or carpentry.

If you can read and write, you'll get to work indoors— but if you're caught misbehaving, you will be demoted back to ditch-digging.

Bow to me, my feeble subjects!

TEACHER'S PET

If you're a teacher's pet at school, you'd make a great PRINCIPALIS. Only the better soldiers are chosen to be a principalis. Their role is to choose who gets put on sentry duty (see page 55) and to help the centurions (see page 44). Like a clique of goody two-shoes, they all hang out together.

HOW TO BECOME TOP BOSS

If you've got a decent amount of money that you can pay as a bribe—I mean donate to the cause—you can start in a more senior position in of the following roles:

PAIN IN THE BUTT

CENTURIONS oversee a cohort of legionaries. They look down on one another and like to prove that they are superior by hitting soldiers with sticks. Legionaries consider all centurions "dolori posteriori" (pains in the butt).

How did Angus go from being a munifex to a centurion?

Hey, look! I'm a centurion!

No wonder it all went wrong for the Romans.

CREST
to make your superiority really obvious

MEDALS
for bravery in battle

STICK
for whacking legionaries

WANNABE GENERAL

MILITARY TRIBUNES often join the army to further their political careers and get rich. They are brutal and shark-like in their ambition.

PRO LEADER

The PRAEFECTUS CASTORUM is a true professional. The longest-serving centurion in the legion, he is in charge of the day-to-day running of the camp.

BACK-UP BOSS

If anything happens to the big boss (the legate), the TRIBUNUS LATICLAVUS takes over. The post is usually held by a young, rich dude from Rome whose plan is to get a cushy government job.

BIG BOSS

The LEGATE is the boss of the whole legion. Most legates only stay in charge for three or four years because the emperor doesn't want them getting ideas about taking his place.

KNOW YOUR ENEMIES

You don't get to be the biggest, baddest empire in the ancient world without making a few enemies. Get to know your foes:

THE PICTS

CALEDONIA

Antonine Wall

Hadrian's Wall

HIBERNIA

BRITANNIA

Londinium (London)

Thames

These vicious warriors are from Caledonia (Scotland). They are nicknamed the "Picts" (meaning "painted") because of their tattoos.

★ HP: 80
★ WEAPONS: spears and simple shields
★ WEAKNESSES: fighting in open areas

★ SPECIAL ABILITIES:
Emerging out of the fog and hacking legionaries to bits before disappearing just as quickly.

THE GERMANS

★ HP: 76
★ WEAPONS: throwing axes, spears
★ WEAKNESSES: habit of fighting each other

There are many different tribes in Germania, each bringing their own style of blood-lust and violence. However, they are all huge, hairy and ferocious. They prefer to fight in boggy forests which, conveniently for them, is what most of Germania is covered with.

★ SPECIAL ABILITIES:

Hurling themselves at the Roman lines in a savage battle charge. Try not to get captured, because they use prisoners as human sacrifices. German tribes can be bribed with a wagon of wine to kill anyone ut you.

Yikes! Is that a man or a monster?

THE JUDEANS

★ **HP:** 74
★ **WEAPONS:** swords, knowledge of the law
★ **WEAKNESSES:** disagreeing with one another

The people of Judea were made citizens of Rome in 66 CE. But not everyone is happy about this. Many Judeans complain about being ruled by Rome. Others simply rebel by killing Roman legionaries.

★ SPECIAL ABILITIES:

Judeans know Roman laws inside out, and keep the emperor busy by protesting against Roman law.

THE BERBERS

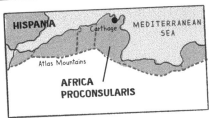

HISPANIA
MEDITERRANEAN SEA
Carthage
Atlas Mountains
AFRICA PROCONSULARIS

★ HP: 79
★ WEAPONS: light javelins
★ WEAKNESSES:
   unable to scale walls
   and attack forts

The Berbers of North Africa are excellent horsemen. They can ride their horses without saddles or bridles, leaving their hands free to throw pointy things at Romans.

★ SPECIAL ABILITIES:

Berbers have very light javelins that can travel further than a Roman pilium. They can stay just out of range of a legionary's spear, while firing weapons at the Roman ranks.

OUCH!

THE DACIANS

> I'm glad I wore this helmet!

Map labels: Aquincum (Budapest), GERMANIA MAGNA, Danube, DACIA, Drobeta, ADRIATIC SEA

★ **HP**: 81
★ **WEAPONS**: lances, bows, hooks and swords
★ **WEAKNESSES**: none

The Dacians (from modern-day Romania) have joined up with the Sarmatians* to fight against Rome.

* Note: that's the Sar-mat-ians, not Sa-mari-tans. There's nothing good about these professional killers.

★ SPECIAL ABILITIES:

The Dacians and the Sarmatians make a terrible twosome. Dacians attack with hooks and clubs. Then the Sarmatian cavalry—whose horses and riders both wear armor—charge in with lances for a deadly finishing strike.

THE PARTHIANS

★ **HP:** 84
★ **WEAPONS:** swords on poles, flaming arrows
★ **WEAKNESSES:** arrows are hard to use in close combat

The Parthian army is led by royal warriors who ride magical-looking horses with incredible speed. Their cavalry is called the "cataphracts" and their armored soldiers carry swords on a 10-foot pole that can skewer two legionaries at once.

★ SPECIAL ABILITIES:

The "Parthian shot" is when a Parthian archer fires an arrow over the tail of his horse while making a swift getaway.

If you die, can I have your horse?

WELCOME TO BASE CAMP

You'll be pleased to hear that fighting enemies is just a small part of your job as a Roman soldier. You'll spend most of your time in army base camps, keeping the locals on their best behavior.

Grrr...

Eeek

Each camp has the same layout, so if you move legions, you won't get lost. At the center of every base camp is the PRINCIPIA. This is the main office where the legion's money is held.

I think I'm going to like working here.

Around the edges are the BARRACKS, where you and your fellow soldiers sleep. Eight soldiers share two small rooms— one for sleeping and one for storage. It's pretty cosy, so bad luck if you get stuck with a snorer.

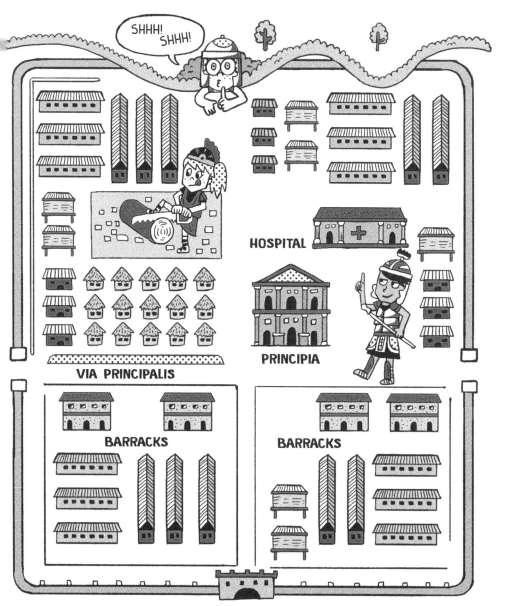

HOSPITAL

PRINCIPIA

VIA PRINCIPALIS

BARRACKS

BARRACKS

PRAETORIAN GATE

BASE CAMP MAP

YOUR DAILY ROUTINE

This is how your day in camp usually goes:

BATHROOM BREAK

Soldiers must be up and dressed before dawn. Bathing and even going to the bathroom are social activities for Romans, so this is your chance to have a chat with your friends while on the toilet. Use the shared sponge on a stick to wipe!

Why does this pork have tiny claws?

Hurry up with the sponge!

EAT BREAKFAST

Cheese and cold meat are a standard breakfast in the Roman army. Hopefully your military tribune (see page 45) will check the quality of the food before serving it.

PARADE

After breakfast, you'll have to line up in a parade. A roll-call will be taken and notices will be read out.

GUARD A GATE

One of the main tasks at camp is sentry duty. You could be on guard at a gate, on the ramparts, by the stores or the principia. Sentry duty is pretty boring unless you've got an interesting view.

HOUSEWORK

Your parents aren't around to clean up after you now. It's your job to clean the toilets, sweep the yard and boil water for the bath house. If you want easier jobs, bribe your centurion.

STILL MORE TRAINING

Remember those smooth moves you learned during your training? You have to keep practicing! Nothing less than perfect performances all-around will please your centurion. Here are the different types of training you will be ordered to do:

CAMPUS

What the army call "campus" is a day spent in the field practicing marching, fighting in formation, mock-fighting another unit, or swimming in a nearby lake or river.

FASTER!

BASILICA OR LUDUS

"Basilica" or "ludus" is a day inside, either in the drill hall or the amphitheater. You'll do exercises such as fighting your old enemy the wooden post, or getting into battle-gear as quickly as possible.

DINNER DUTY

Grub's up! Legionaries are better fed than the rest of the empire's citizens— it's no good having hungry and weak soldiers. Meat, cheese, bread and beer are all on the menu.

BURP...

FINAL INSPECTION

The evening is a chance to catch up with mail and packages from home, as well as get your gear ready for one of the endless inspections.

BATH TIME

When legionaries get time off, they go to the bath house. It's time to get clean, play dice and gossip about your bosses.

He puts leaves around his head and suddenly he's Mr. Important.

PREPARE FOR WAR!

Before you leave base camp to go to war, there are some final preparations you should make:

1. WRITE LETTERS

There's a good chance you'll die, so you might want to take the opportunity to write to your family or your secret girlfriend or boyfriend.

2. TOUGHEN UP

If you've been living in a permanent camp for a long time, you may have gotten a bit soft. Your general may make you camp in a field for a couple of weeks to toughen you up and prepare you for what is to come. Some winters the training is so intense that soldiers' hands drop off from frostbite!

WHAAA!!!

3. FATTEN UP

Going to war burns a lot of energy, but there often isn't as much food available when you're on the move. So try to eat a lot before leaving base camp.

4. PRACTICE DIGGING

Dig, dig and then dig a bit more. Digging is a valuable skill when you're on the move with the Roman army. You'll dig trenches around camps, ditches to stop enemy cavalry, and other digging activities.

5. PEP TALK

Once you're ready, the commander will address all the troops. He'll explain the purpose of the battle and, most importantly, what treasure he wants you to seize.

MAKE A BATTLE PLAN

When the Roman army decides to fight an enemy, there's no messing around. They don't bother with BLOCKADES (cutting off an enemy's supplies) or SANCTIONS (refusing to trade with them). The tried and tested Roman battle plan is, simply:

CRUSH THE ENEMY INTO DUST.

ROMAN ARMY

ENEMY

I want a pair of those sandals!

The GENERALS will decide what your enemy cares most about (such as defending their capital city) and aim straight for it. Any angry armies that try to stop the Roman army from moving forward will be chopped to pieces.

WAIT!

ENEMY FINELY SLICED

I'm not dead meat, I'm stir fry!

To take over an enemy's capital city, the Roman army forms a COLUMN OF MARCH. The exact arrangement of the column of march depends a bit on what type of enemy the army is fighting but the classic column of march is like a human freight train.

WALK TO WAR

Most Roman soldiers get to the battlefield by walking. Form a column of march for safety so there are still some soldiers left when you reach the battlefield.

HEADS UP!

PATH CLEARERS

At the front of the column of march are SCOUTS. They clear the path for the rest of the soldiers and check woodlands for enemies hiding in the bushes.

BRUTAL BACK-UP

Behind the scouts come the COVERING FORCE. If scouts do bump into an enemy trap, they'll be protected by the covering force—heavily armed infantry capable of fighting off enemy attackers.

Has anyone lost a sandal? This one has a foot in it.

ROAD FIXERS

A team of ENGINEERS AND NAVVIES patch up and improve the road super-speedily just before the rest of the army walks over it. Avoid if you suffer from work-related stress.

Let's put Tacillus' tent in that smelly bog!

This will have to do!

CAMP SITE PICKERS

After the covering force come the PIONEERS. They are responsible for deciding where the camp should be built that night, and for marking out where each tent and ditch should be dug.

LUGGAGE HOLD

Food and supplies for the entire army are carried in the BAGGAGE TRAIN. Also carried here are the SIEGE ENGINES that are used to break down the walls and doors of the enemy's city. This is the part of the column that your enemies will most want to attack.

Oops! There goes dessert!

What are those idiots doing?!

SAFE AND SOUND

Right in the middle of the column are the general, the cavalry and the officers. From here, the general can quickly get to the front or back of the column to deal with any problems during the march.

LEGIONARY SANDWICH

The column of march is mostly made up of legionaries. At the front go the EAGLES (soldiers carrying a metal eagle on a tall pole) and the TRUMPETERS. Behind the legionaries are the mules, carrying the soldiers' personal belongings and tents.

THE TAIL END

At the back of the column are the SUPERNUMERIES (allies whom the Romans sometimes bring along). Behind them are the REARGUARD, a group of heavily armed infantry and cavalry soldiers who fight off any enemies that sneak up from behind.

LIFE ON CAMPAIGN

HOME AWAY FROM HOME

If your CAMPAIGN, or mission, is to fight an enemy far away from base camp, you'll need to set up temporary camps along the march. They will feel like your home away from home, because every Roman camp is identical. As long as you build them properly, you'll be more than comfortable.

It takes three hours to complete a camp. Everyone has their own task. You might be a ditch digger or a wall builder.

PITCH IN

You'll be sharing an oilskin tent called a papilio with eight other soldiers—even more cosy than your barracks back home. If the weather is cold, the ceiling of your papilio can be kept low, so the air inside warms up quickly with the body heat (and gas) of all the men inside.

CAMP FOOD

How do you keep meat fresh on a long march? Easy, you make it march with you. A herd of cattle follows the legion to be slaughtered one by one for steaks. Otherwise, dinner is mostly grain: boiled grain, mashed grain, grain porridge...hope you like grain!

Storming, or attacking, a city is an essential skill in the Roman army. It can also go badly, so make sure you study the best techniques beforehand!

HOW TO STORM CITIES AND VANQUISH ENEMIES
BY LEONTIUS SACCUS SITIUS

BESTSELLER
OVER 10 COPIES SOLD!

There's no point marching hundreds of miles to an enemy city, if you haven't got what it takes to completely DESTROY it. Have no fear! Follow these SIMPLE TIPS, and storm that city like a pro!

TALK IT THROUGH

Ask yourself, why are you storming a city in the first place? Because of the MONEY and POWER you'll gain! Why damage the city you want to take over when you could NEGOTIATE or argue for the city to surrender itself? (It helps if your troops are seen to be preparing for violence in the background.)

Give us 5,000 denarii or we'll send in The Unit.

WAIT IT OUT

Build WALLS and dig TRENCHES around the city to trap your enemy inside. But be prepared for a long wait— BESIEGED soldiers have been known to eat each other before they surrender!

Oh no! They're eating their sandals

Wait until they start nibbling their toes.

GET VIOLENT

If peaceful methods don't work, it's time to get violent. Choose from different ARTILLERY (heavy weapons) depending on the effect you're after:

FIRE ARROWS

Massive BOWS that fire enormous ARROWS have the advantage of being able to skewer a human being like a cocktail sausage on a stick. They're so sharp, they even go through armor.

THROW ROCKS

A CATAPULT throws huge rocks that can smash down walls. With good aim you can also knock enemies' heads right off their shoulders.

GO UNDERGROUND

Getting inside a city can be hard work. One effective way to collapse a city's walls is by DIGGING TUNNELS underneath them. This is how it's done:

First, prop up the foundations of the city wall with wooden posts. Dig a tunnel directly underneath the wall. When the tunnel is finished, set fire to the wooden posts as you leave. The posts will burn and the wall they are supporting will collapse so your army can then storm in.

CAUTION!

If the defending army figures out where you are tunneling, they might dig a tunnel of their own. Angry bears and wasps will be sent into the tunnel to attack your soldiers!

SMASH THE GATES

Use a BATTERING RAM to break your way in through the city gates. The ram is a big log of wood with an iron ram's head on the front. When you pull it back on its frame and let go, it will swing forward and smash through just about anything.

Oh, I thought you said "bleating lamb."

RAMP IT UP

Build a big SIEGE MOUND, or ramp, out of earth and logs along the city wall. Now your army can walk up the ramp and drop over the city wall. But watch out! The enemy might collapse your mound by digging underneath it.

TOWER OVER

A SIEGE TOWER is like an armored apartment building. Simply wheel your siege tower up to the city wall. Let soldiers with ARTILLERY take out any enemies defending the wall. Then send in the rest of your soldiers. They'll climb up the tower's stairs and onto the wall. Once inside, Roman troops will get on with LOOTING and MURDERING every living thing—even the pets!

USE A LADDER

If you're in a rush, you can just use a LADDER. But be careful—it's easy to make rookie mistakes. If your ladder goes all the way to the top of the wall, the enemy can simply shove it over from above. If you place it at too much of an angle, it might snap under the weight of the soldiers climbing it.

METELLA'S GUIDE TO LOOTING

Hi guys! I'm back with another how to, and this time it's how to get the best stuff when you go looting! Attacking a city is the best opportunity to get an amazing haul of new things. Here are my top tips for what to grab!

STASH SOME CASH

Number one, obvs, is cash. Stash those gold and silver coins. But remember, you'll have to hand in anything you get to the general who will share it out equally.

STEAL SOME ART

By "art" I mean fancy paintings, statues, tapestries—anything gorgeous. Most of this stuff will be given to the emperor, but if you're lucky, you might get a piece for your dorm!

Hey Kate, it's you!

A rare coin!

74

GRAB SOME GARB

Who doesn't love new clothes?! Look out for clothes that are dyed Tyrian purple. This super expensive dye is made from sea snail slime and makes even the oldest hand-me-downs worth pinching.

SELL YOUR ENEMY

One of the most popular things to loot is people. Enemies can be sold as property for a nice profit.

Finally, remember that if your legion collects enough goodies and takes them back to the emperor, he might give everyone a tax break and then you'll be sooo popular!

Shall we catch that guy?

HOPE YOU ENJOYED READING MY RECOMMENDATIONS! LOVE YOU GUYS!

Uhhh... you first.

75

Eventually, you'll have to do more than just exercises and stealing stuff. All Roman soldiers must come face to face with their enemy. Then it's time to...

FIGHT!

1. FIND A FIELD

First, THE SCOUTS will go looking for the enemy to figure out the best place to fight. Once a field is chosen, the generals will either wait for extra soldiers to arrive or for a good omen before sending you into battle.

CAW! YOU'RE ALL GOING TO DIE! CAW!

I think that's a bad omen.

2. LINE UP STRAIGHT

The entire army will line up in formation, with the AUXILIA in front (see page 32). The auxilia are not highly valued, so a general will try to get the job done with the auxilia and without losing any legionaries.

3. DUCK!

The enemy will begin firing arrows, so keep your shield up and your head down, or you might get an arrow in the eye. At this point, the Roman army brings out the SCORPIONS—large crossbows that are powerful enough to skewer three people with a single shot.

4. CHAAARGE!!!

After the first shots have been fired, the real COMBAT begins.

CREEP FORWARD

At first, all soldiers slowly walk forward together in a line. About a dozen feet from the enemy, soldiers draw their swords, and it's time to...

CHAAAARGE!!!!!

BODY-SLAM

The front row of legionaries start by body-slamming their opponents to the ground. Someone in the row behind will then stab the enemy.

SPILL YOUR GUTS

Legionaries have a special way of hacking into their enemies. A hard punch with the shield is followed by a stab to the belly. A twist of the sword will create a giant wound and out of that will spill the enemy's guts. Then on to the next one.

TIME OUT

If the fighting is still raging after 10 minutes, soldiers in the FRONT LINE will need a break. They signal to a soldier in the second row to take their place by lifting their shield and stepping back.

5. STAY ALIVE FOR THE PRIZE

After the fighting is over, it's time to tend to any injuries before you start LOOTING. That's assuming the Romans won, of course. If things went badly, the wounded are left to fend for themselves while everyone else hotfoots it back to the safety of camp.

This would look gorgeous on me!

LOOT THE BODIES

Immediately after the battle, soldiers will grab a few bits from those who died on the battlefield. Gold brooches, belts and money pouches are great take-home gifts. But it isn't only the standing soldiers who deserve WINNINGS. Those being patched up are also owed their share.

Give it back! I'm not dead yet.

TAKE A SOUVENIR

Enemy heads make a popular souvenir. German and Gallic auxilia have been seen doing battle with **ENEMY HEADS** in their teeth so they don't lose them. Human skulls can be preserved and turned into drinking cups.

A lovely addition to my Roman tea set.

The operation was a success!

That was my good leg.

SEE A DOCTOR

Compared to the rest of the ancient world, Roman medicine was quite good and army medics could conduct life-saving surgeries. Stapling together severed tendons, removing barbed arrowheads from flesh and **AMPUTATING LIMBS** were all in a day's work.

VICTORY!

WOOOHOO!!

The Romans show their might once again! If the emperor agrees your battle met all the criteria, you and your soldiers will enjoy a TRIUMPH, or victory parade, through the streets of Rome.
The criteria includes:

✔ At least 5,000 enemies have been killed,

✔ The battle has ended the campaign,

✔ The campaign has increased the glory of the Roman empire.

Sadly, not everyone gets to go to Rome because troops are still needed to defend the borders of the empire. Priority is given to legionaries who are about to retire, or who were so badly injured that they are allowed to leave the army.

HOW TO CELEBRATE A VICTORY, ROMAN STYLE

Thanks, Jupiter!

Yeah, thanks a lot!

✔ Deck the city in flowers.

✔ Gather the legions and march together through the Porta Triumphalis ("triumph gate"), a special gate used for victory events.

✔ Parade through the streets singing songs and holding spears decorated with leaves.

✔ Carry your general through the crowds in a fancy chariot. Paint his face red, in the style of the god Jupiter.

✔ At the temple of Jupiter, sacrifice white oxen in thanks for Jupiter's protection. Say your prayers.

✔ After the ceremony, party for at least a week.

83

I'M A LEGIONARY, GET ME OUT OF HERE!

Have you had enough of bloody battles and camp life?
Here are four different ways you can get out of the army:

1. GET INJURED

If you're injured in battle, and are no longer of any use to the army, you'll get an honorable discharge.

I hurt my toe. Can I leave now?

2. BEHAVE BADLY

If you commit a serious crime you will be beaten and discharged dishonorably. This means no pension and no living in Rome.

Come back here, thief!

3. DO YOUR TIME

Complete 25 years' service, and you can leave the army with your head held high and a pocket full of cash.

Was I not a good soldier?

4. FALL DOWN DEAD

Another way out, of course, is death. This will limit your future somewhat.

R.I.P.
LEONTIUS
VALIANT SOLDIER
WHO SERVED
25 YEARS IN
THE ROMAN ARMY
AND HAS NOW
OFFICIALLY COMPLETED
HIS SERVICE.

SO, DO YOU REALLY WANT TO BE A
ROMAN SOLDIER?

Well done, you three!
You managed to survive
the brutal exercises,
the daily grind and various
hostile enemies without so much
as a scratch on you!

Should I tell the
emperor he has
three new recruits?

86

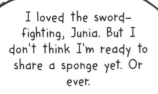

I loved the sword-fighting, Junia. But I don't think I'm ready to share a sponge yet. Or ever.

Junia! You should have seen me in the cavalry—I was amazing! But I'm exhausted now. I just want to go home and watch TV. What about you, Angus?

I'm sorry, Kate. You'll have to tell Mom and Dad I'm never coming back. I think I've found my calling as a Praetorian Guard.

IF WARRIOR LIFE APPEALS, BUT YOU'RE NOT CONVINCED YOU'RE **THE LEGIONARY TYPE**, TURN TO PAGE 96 FOR OTHER ANCIENT JOB OPTIONS!

CALEDONIA

PICTS

HIBERNIA

NORTH SEA

IX

XX
BRITANNIA

II   Londinium
      (London)
      Thames

GERMANS

GERMANIA
MAGNA

XXII

VI

X

Germania
Inferior

Elbe

Seine

VII

Lutetia
(Paris)

Germania
Superior

XVII

Rhine

Danube

XV

ATLANTIC OCEAN

GALLIA

Argentoratum
(Strasbourg)

XVI

VII

HISPANIA

Tagus

ADRIATIC SEA

Rome

ITALIA

MEDITERRANEAN SEA

Carthage

III

AFRICA
PROCONSULARIS

Atlas Mountains

BERBERS

N

SCALE

310 miles

88

ROMAN EMPIRE MAP

The dotted lines mark the edge of the Roman Empire in 100 CE.

Roman numerals mark where each legion was based. The names of countries are written in Latin, the official language of the Roman Empire.

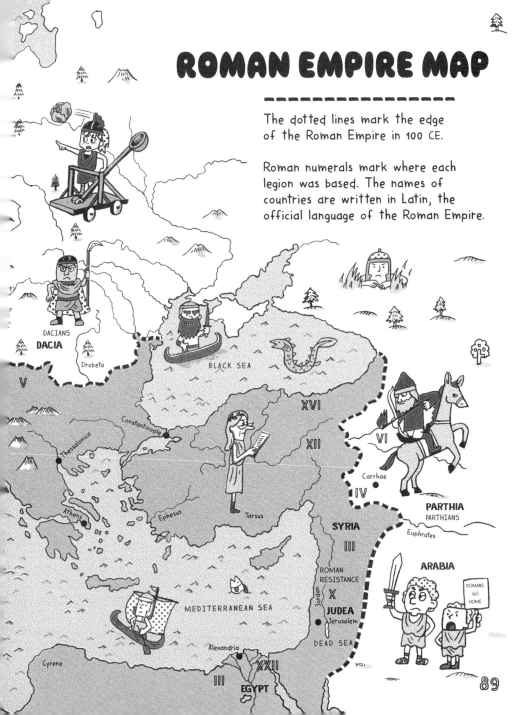

DACIANS
DACIA

Drobeta

BLACK SEA

V

Constantinople

Thessalonica

XVI

XII

VI

Carrhae

Athens

Ephesus

Tarsus

IV

PARTHIA
PARTHIANS

SYRIA

Euphrates

III

ARABIA

ROMAN
RESISTANCE

X

JUDEA
Jerusalem

ROMANS
GO
HOME

MEDITERRANEAN SEA

DEAD SEA

Cyrene

Alexandria

XXII

III

EGYPT

89

GLOSSARY

ARTILLERY weapons (such as bows, slings and catapults) that fire objects (such as arrows or rocks) at the enemy

ASSASSINATE to murder someone famous or important for political or religious reasons

AUXILIA soldiers who were not Roman citizens. The name means "helpers."

BARRACKS a large building or group of buildings where soldiers live

BERBERS people from modern-day North Africa

BLOCKADE stopping food and other supplies from entering a place

CAMPAIGN a series of military operations such as battles or sieges that have a particular overall goal, such as taking over a country

CAVALRY soldiers who fight on horseback

CENTURION an officer in the Roman army

COLUMN OF MARCH the order in which soldiers and engineers travel towards a battle or siege

DACIANS people from the area of modern-day Romania

DECIMATION a punishment in which one out of every ten soldiers is executed

DESERTER a soldier who runs away from the army

EMPEROR the ruler of the Roman empire

FLOGGING to beat someone with a whip or stick as a punishment

GERMANS people from the area of modern-day Germany

GUERILLA a member of a small group of fighters who use tactics such as ambushes and raids, instead of fighting in formal battles

HOSTILE   unfriendly

IMMUNE   a soldier in the Roman army with special duties

INFANTRY   soldiers who fight on foot

JAVELIN   a spear that is designed to be thrown

JUDEANS   people from the area of modern-day Israel and Palestine

KNUCKLEDUSTER   a weapon worn over the knuckles to increase the power of a punch

LEGATE   the commander of a legion

MILITARY TRIBUNE   one of the senior officers in a legion

MUNIFEX   the lowest-level soldier in the army

NEGOTIATE   to try to achieve agreement by discussion

OMEN   a sign or signal of good or bad luck

PAPILIO   the tent that legionaries use when on a campaign

PARTHIANS   people from a powerful kingdom to the east of the Roman empire

PATRIOTISM   passionate love and support of one's country

PENSION   money paid to people after they stop working because of old age

PICT   people who lived in the area that is modern-day Scotland

PILUM   the spear that legionaries use to throw at enemies

PIONEERS   soldiers who are responsible for deciding where the camp site should be built

PRAEFECTUS CASTORUM   an officer who is in charge of the day-to-day running of the army camp

PRAETORIAN GUARD   soldiers who work for the emperor in Rome

PRINCIPIA   the building at the center of a Roman army camp

PROMOTION upgrading someone to a higher rank

REARGUARD the soldiers who go at the back of the column of march to protect against attacks from behind

RECRUIT someone who has recently joined the army and is not fully trained

RETIREMENT when someone stops working, usually due to old age

SAMARTIANS a group of fierce fighters from north of the Black Sea

SANCTION a punishment, particularly when one country refuses to trade with another country

SCABBARD the case for a sword

SIEGE when an army surrounds a town or building, cutting off supplies, in order to make the people inside surrender

SIEGE ENGINE a device designed to break down or get around heavy doors or walls

SKIRMISH a fight between a small group of troops, often before a larger, formal battle begins

SPATHA the sword that Roman cavalry used

SPOUSE a husband or wife

TRIBUNUS LATICLAVUS the second-in-command of a legion

TRIREME a Roman warship

VANQUISH to defeat thoroughly

VETERAN an experienced soldier

ROMAN NUMERALS

In Roman times they didn't use the same numbers that we use today. The numbers we use originated in India around 500-600 CE, and came to Europe via the writings of Middle Eastern mathematicians. Here are the numerals that a legionary would have been familiar with:

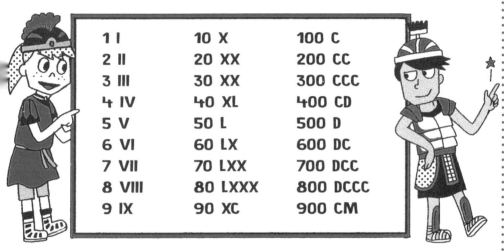

1 I	10 X	100 C
2 II	20 XX	200 CC
3 III	30 XX	300 CCC
4 IV	40 XL	400 CD
5 V	50 L	500 D
6 VI	60 LX	600 DC
7 VII	70 LXX	700 DCC
8 VIII	80 LXXX	800 DCCC
9 IX	90 XC	900 CM

When writing a number that isn't on this list (such as **58** or **2019**), you write it in the same way that we do, in columns for the ones, tens, hundreds and thousands. Where there would be a zero in our numbers, just leave it blank.

For example, **2019** is like this:

2	0	1	9
MM		X	IX

So, **MMXIX**.

Or, to write **58**, it's **L (50)** and **VIII (8)**. So, **LVIII**.

INDEX

If you don't want to be a **ROMAN SOLDIER**, you might want to think about becoming a **VIKING**. Both girls and boys may apply.